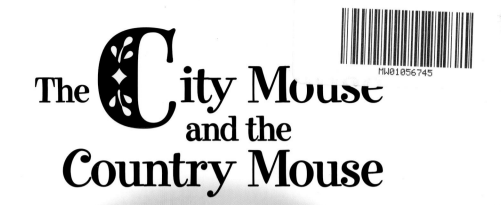

The City Mouse and the Country Mouse

A friendly brown field mouse named Jethro lived in a cozy little cabin that he'd built on his own at the edge of a quiet meadow in the countryside. He lived a simple, peaceful life, and took pleasure in the practical routine of his daily tasks and friendly visits with neighbors.

Mimsy was Jethro's cousin. She lived in the nearby bustling city. Mimsy liked all the action and activity the big city offered, and thought that it was the most exciting place to live.

One day, Jethro wrote a letter to his cousin, and invited Mimsy to come and visit him in the country. He thought that it would be wonderful to see his cousin again and have a proper visit.

When Mimsy received Jethro's letter, she thought that it would be a great idea, too! Mimsy used to visit often with her family when they were little mice, but the cousins hadn't seen each other in a very long time. She promptly wrote Jethro back to say that she was on her way. Then, Mimsy quickly packed a bag and dressed in one of her prettiest outfits, and set off for the country.

Meanwhile, Jethro prepared his humble home for the arrival of his guest. He swept the floor and tidied. He put aside some of his finest cheese to serve, and gathered some fresh berries from the part of the meadow where they tasted the very best.

The day Mimsy was to arrive, the weather was beautiful! Jethro decided that a backyard picnic was the best way to enjoy a wonderful day in the country. He packed up the special cheese and juicy berries, and placed them on a tray on a blanket in the grass behind his home.

Mimsy will be so pleased! Jethro thought.

He couldn't think of a better way to spend their visit! It was so warm and sunny out, that he decided to stretch out on the blanket and wait for Mimsy there. Before he settled in, he posted a quick note on his front door that read:

Welcome Mimsy! I'm waiting for you out back!

When Mimsy arrived, she read Jethro's note and went around to the picnic spot at the back of the house.

"Jethro, it's so good to see you!" she said as she hugged her cousin hello.

"It's wonderful to see you too, Mimsy!" Jethro said with a smile. "You must be hungry after your trip! Please, sit down and have a bite to eat."

Mimsy's tummy growled. She was very hungry! She glanced at the blanket and the food on the tray, and saw that there were no chairs and no table. The only food she could see was some cheese and a few berries. Was this really all her cousin had to eat? Mimsy was wearing a pretty dress, and was afraid to ruin it by sitting on the blanket. But she also didn't want to be rude.

Mimsy sat down carefully so as not to ruin her dress, and ate the cheese and berries with her cousin.

"You know, Jethro, in the city, we have all kinds of things to eat! Things you've probably never even seen out here! Cupcakes and candy, and all sorts of exotic treats from around the world!" said Mimsy.

Jethro's eyes widened.

"That does sound nice, Mimsy!" he admitted.

"Why don't you come back with me, and visit the city!" Mimsy cried. "I'll show you how to really live!"

Jethro loved his home in the country, but he was also curious about the city and had never visited before.

A little visit wouldn't hurt, he thought. *Besides, I have always wanted to see what the big city is really like.*

"Ok, Mimsy," Jethro said. "Let's go!"

Mimsy thought this was wonderful news. She was more excited than ever! Jethro was really going to love the city—she was certain of it! They finished up their modest lunch and set off toward the big city.

Jethro could hear the noise of the city before they could even see it. It began as a faint din, and as they approached, the sounds grew louder and seemed to multiply! Jethro heard all kinds of unfamiliar noises.

"Follow me, Jethro!" cried Mimsy as she led the way down the side of a busy street.

Jethro was right behind her. There were so many things to look at, it was almost too much! Suddenly, a car on the street slammed on its brakes and honked loudly. Jethro jumped in surprise and let out a squeak.

"Oh, don't worry about that, Jethro," said Mimsy. "It's just a car! As long as you stay out of its way, you'll be just fine!"

Jethro smiled meekly, but he wasn't so sure!

They zigzagged through streets and down alleyways, until at long last Mimsy disappeared through a narrow opening in a very large, tall house. Jethro had never seen such a huge house before!

"Come this way! It's time to eat!" called Mimsy.

Jethro followed Mimsy through the house toward the dining room. Everything was so large!

"I've been living here for a few months now," explained Mimsy. "They have the best meals! Believe me, we aren't going to bed hungry!"

The two mice entered the empty dining room. Jethro couldn't believe his eyes! Before them lay the most lavish feast he had ever seen in his whole life. There was a huge roast, a fruit platter, and dishes all along the length of the table as far as the eye could see.

"Dig in!" declared Mimsy, as she scurried up to a dish and ate a piece of raspberry tart.

"This is delicious!" gushed Jethro, as he stuffed an olive in his mouth. "I've never seen anything like it!"

Just as the words left his mouth, there was a loud bark, followed by an even louder bark, and the sound of hurried steps.

Jethro stopped chewing at once, and stood up on his toes to sniff the air.

Mimsy didn't waste a second.

"Run, Jethro!" she cried as she scurried toward the opening in the wall they had first come from.

Startled and suddenly very afraid, Jethro took off after Mimsy.

The sounds grew louder and louder until two dogs burst into the dining room and began sniffing around the floor and table. Mimsy and Jethro cowered inside the hole in the wall. One of the dogs came right up to the hole and stuck its nose in, sniffing madly.

"Follow me," Mimsy whispered to Jethro.

When they were safely away from the dining room and the dogs, Jethro let out a sigh of relief, and Mimsy giggled with laughter.

"That was close!" she said.

"Mimsy, the city sure is exciting!" said Jethro. "But I would really like to go home now. I really don't think this is the place for a country mouse like me."

"I understand, Jethro," said Mimsy. "I can still visit you in the country every now and then though, right?"

"You're always welcome in the country, Mimsy!" said Jethro. "Please, visit any time."

And with that, Mimsy led Jethro to the outskirts of the city, where Jethro continued the rest of the way home by himself.

The following morning, Jethro woke up to a brand-new day in the fresh country air. It was safe and peaceful, and best of all, he was home!